This book belongs to

Franklin's Friendship Treasury

This book includes the following stories:
Franklin Has a Sleepover first published in 1996
Franklin's Bad Day first published in 1996
Franklin's New Friend first published in 1997
Franklin's Secret Club first published in 1998

Kids Can Press acknowledges the financial support of the Ontario Arts Council, the Canada Council for the Arts and the Government of Canada, through the BPIDP, for our publishing activity.

Published in Canada by
Kids Can Press Ltd.
29 Birch Avenue
Toronto, ON M4V 1E2

Published in the U.S. by
Kids Can Press Ltd.
4500 Witmer Estates
Niagara Falls, NY 14305–1386

Printed in Hong Kong by Wing King Tong Company Limited

CM 00 0 9 8 7 6 5 4 3 2 1

Canadian Cataloguing in Publication Data

Bourgeois, Paulette
Franklin's friendship treasury

ISBN 1-55074-872-6

I. Clark, Brenda. II. Title.

PS8553.O85477F855 2000   jC813'.54   C99-932727-5
PZ7.B6654Fxg 2000

Kids Can Press is a Nelvana company

Franklin's FRIENDSHIP *Treasury*

Paulette Bourgeois • Brenda Clark

Kids Can Press

Contents

Franklin Has a Sleepover

Written by Paulette Bourgeois
Illustrated by Brenda Clark

FRANKLIN could count by twos and tie his shoes. He could zip zippers and button buttons. He could even sleep alone in his small, dark shell. So Franklin thought he was ready for his first sleepover. He asked his mother if Bear could stay overnight.

"All right," said Franklin's mother. "But where will Bear sleep?"

Franklin's room was small for a turtle *and* a bear.

"We could sleep in the living room," suggested Franklin. "And we could have a campfire outside and ..."

"Wait a minute!" laughed Franklin's mother. "You haven't even asked Bear yet."

Bear did a happy dance after Franklin called.

"May I please go?" he asked.

His parents worried that the two friends would keep each other awake all night.

"We'll sleep," promised Bear.

Then they wondered if he would feel homesick.

"Not me!" said Bear.

So his parents said yes.

Bear called Franklin. "I can come! I can come!" he shouted.

Franklin could hardly wait. Bear wouldn't arrive until after supper, and Franklin had just finished lunch. So he sorted all his toys and picked Bear's favourites. He made sure there was enough to eat. He even tidied his room. Franklin wanted everything to be just right for his first sleepover.

Bear was excited, too. He couldn't decide what to bring and what to leave behind. He filled an enormous bag with toys, books, a pillow, a sleeping bag, a puzzle and a flashlight. He packed slippers, a toothbrush and a snack. He put his bunny on top of the bag. And every hour he asked if it was time to go.

After supper, Franklin sat by the window, waiting for his friend. Finally, Bear and his parents arrived.

"Have a good time," they said. Bear gave them each a great big hug.

"We're camping in the living room," said Franklin.

"Oh, I've never done that before," said Bear.

He laid out his sleeping bag and Franklin made a tent from a tablecloth.

"This is going to be so much fun," giggled Bear.

They played all their favourite games. Before long it was dark outside.

"How about a campfire?" asked Franklin's father.

"With marshmallows?" Bear licked his lips.

"And hot dogs too," said Franklin's mother.

Franklin's father told Bear and Franklin what to do. They gathered sticks and twigs at the edge of the woods and helped to lay the fire. They filled a bucket with sand and another with water.

"I'll light the fire," said Franklin's mother.

There was a crackle, and sparks jumped into the air.

"I went to camp," said Franklin's father. "We used to sing while the fire was burning."

He sang in a clear, low voice. By the end of the song, Franklin and Bear had learned all the words. The frogs in the pond were croaking, and the owl in the woods was hooting.

Franklin and Bear toasted marshmallows and roasted hot dogs. Bear had two of everything. Then for a long, long time they sat quietly, watching the stars.

Franklin yawned and Bear rubbed his eyes.

"Time to put out the fire and go inside," said Franklin's father.

When Franklin and Bear were ready for bed, Franklin's parents gave them both a glass of water and a good-night hug.

"Sleep tight," they said, turning off the light.

The two friends lay still for a moment. Then Bear turned on his flashlight.

"Franklin?" he whispered. "I don't feel good."

"Did you eat too much?" asked Franklin.

"No," sniffed Bear. A tear ran down his cheek.

"What's wrong then?"

Bear looked around. "I miss my room."

"Oh," said Franklin. Then he had an idea. "Bring your bed and come with me. We can sleep in my room."

Bear found a cosy spot and snuggled into his sleeping bag. After a moment, he turned on his flashlight again.

"What's wrong now?" Franklin asked.

"My mother always says good night to my bunny," whispered Bear.

So Franklin gave the bunny a hug. "Good night, Bunny. Good night, Bear," he said.

Soon they were fast asleep.

The next morning, Franklin's father made them a special breakfast.

"Did you have a nice sleepover?" asked Franklin's mother.

"It was wonderful," said Bear. "Thank you. Next time, may Franklin come to my house?"

"Of course," Franklin's parents laughed.
Franklin did his own happy dance.
"And, Bear," said Franklin, tapping his shell, "don't worry about where I will sleep. I always bring my own cosy bed with me!"

Franklin's Bad Day

Written by Paulette Bourgeois
Illustrated by Brenda Clark

FRANKLIN loved to play outside in winter. He could skate forwards and backwards. He liked to catch snowflakes on his tongue and make angels in the snow. But today was different. Franklin was having a very bad day.

It started in the morning. Franklin was grumpy when he woke up.

"That's a grouchy face," teased his father.

"Yes it is," said Franklin. He crossed his arms and frowned.

"Would you like a nice breakfast?" asked his mother.

"No!" said Franklin.

His mother made breakfast anyway.

Franklin stared out the window. Heavy grey clouds pushed across the sky.

"It's even a bad day outside," grumbled Franklin.

He picked at his food.

For the rest of the morning, nothing went right.
Franklin knocked over his juice and broke his favourite cup. He couldn't find his marbles, and the last piece of his puzzle was missing.
Franklin slammed a door and stomped his feet.
"You seem awfully cranky," said his mother.
"I am not!" shouted Franklin.

Just then, Bear knocked on the door. Franklin peeked out.

"Do you want to make a snowman or ride on my sled?" asked Bear.

Franklin sighed. "I don't want to do *anything*."

"Please?" Bear said.

"Fresh air will do you good," said his parents. "Out you go with Bear."

They handed Franklin his hat and mittens.

Franklin pouted as he bundled up and went outside.

SOLD

The two friends walked along the path near Otter's house.

"Let's ask Otter to come," said Bear.

Franklin gave Bear a puzzled look.

"Oh, I forgot," said Bear sadly. "Otter moved away yesterday."

They didn't talk all the way to the hill.

Franklin kneeled at the front of the sled and Bear sat behind him.

Bear gave a push. "Let's go!" he shouted.

The sled glided halfway down the slope. And then it stopped. They had landed on a bare patch.

"Oh no!" wailed Franklin. "What a terrible day!"

NO
SKATING

The hill was no fun, so Beaver suggested they go to the pond.

When they arrived, the pond was roped off.

"No skating today," warned Mr. Mole. "The ice is thin."

Franklin lost his temper. "This is my worstest day ever!"

"There's no such word as worstest," said Beaver.

"There is for me!" said Franklin. "I'm leaving!"

Franklin stormed home.

He threw his skates and his slushy, mushy mittens on the floor.

"Please pick up your things," said his mother.

"NO!" he yelled.

Franklin was sent to his room.

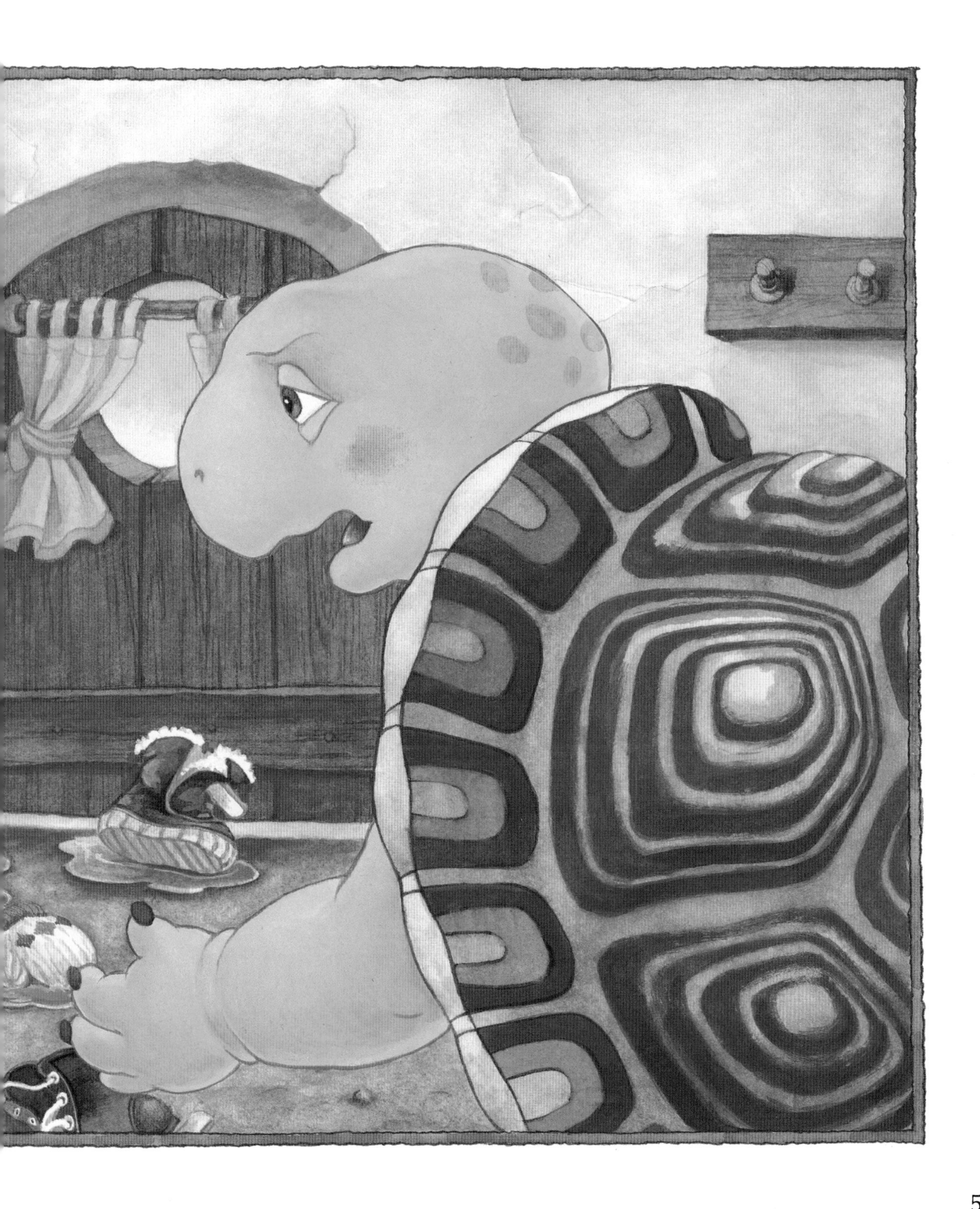

Franklin was so furious that he kicked his castle.

His father came running when he heard the crash. "What's going on in here?"

Franklin lay on the floor and cried.

"Don't worry," said his father. "You can build the castle again."

"But I made that castle with Otter, and she's not here any more," sobbed Franklin.

"Oh, now I understand," said Franklin's father. "You're mad and sad because your friend moved away."

Franklin nodded.

"And you miss her a lot," his father said.

"Yes," agreed Franklin in a small voice.

They hugged each other for a long time.

"Otter and I did lots of things together," said Franklin. "Now we can't."

"You can still be friends," said Franklin's father. "You can share your feelings by calling or writing."

Franklin thought for a moment.

"Do we have a big envelope and some stamps?" he asked.

Franklin spent the rest of the day making a scrapbook for Otter.

He filled it with pictures and drawings of the two friends together.

Near the back, Franklin put a dozen envelopes. He printed his address on each one.

On the last page, he wrote:

Please write to me. Then we can stay friends forever.

As he walked to the mailbox, Franklin felt better.

Snow was falling and it was getting cold enough for the pond to freeze.

Franklin had a feeling that tomorrow would be a good day.

Franklin's New Friend

Written by Paulette Bourgeois
Illustrated by Brenda Clark

FRANKLIN had always lived in the same house in the same town. He had grown up with his friends, and each one had a special place in Franklin's life.

When Franklin wanted to play hide and seek, he called Fox. If Franklin needed a best friend, he called Bear.

Franklin never thought about making friends until a new family moved in down the lane.

Franklin was curious about the newcomers.

He rubbed his eyes as the movers unloaded the furniture. The beds were made for giants, and the lamps were as tall as trees.

When Franklin finally saw the family, he was speechless.

Franklin had never met a moose before. He had heard about moose. He had seen pictures of moose. But he had never actually known one. They were huge. Even the smallest moose was big.

Franklin was so scared that he raced home.

"A moose family moved in!"

"That's nice," said Franklin's mother. "Maybe you'll make a new friend."

Franklin shook his head. "I don't think so."

"I expect you to be nice when you meet someone new," warned his mother.

Franklin scowled.

The next morning, there was a moose in Franklin's classroom.

"Please give a warm welcome to your new classmate," said Mr. Owl.

"Hello, Moose," said the class in unison.
Moose mumbled hello and looked at his feet.
"He doesn't look very friendly," whispered Beaver.

Mr. Owl told the class that Moose had come from a different place, far away.

"Franklin," said Mr. Owl, "I'd like you to be a buddy for Moose."

Franklin tried to smile but he was scared. Moose was so big!

Moose didn't say a word all morning.

At recess, Franklin ran outside with his friends, leaving Moose behind. But Mr. Owl reminded Franklin that he was Moose's buddy.

"Do you want to play?" asked Franklin.

Moose shook his head back and forth.

Franklin was relieved.

During recess, Moose stood alone as Franklin and his friends played soccer.

Fox kicked the ball too hard, and it flew into a tree.

"Now we'll have to get Mr. Owl," groaned Bear.

"I've got it!" cried Moose. He knocked the ball out of the tree and sent it flying to Franklin.

"That was good," said Fox.

"I guess," shrugged Franklin.

Back in the classroom, Mr. Owl asked Franklin and Moose to make a poster for the bake sale.

"I don't need any help," said Franklin.

Mr. Owl talked to Franklin alone. "Try to imagine how Moose feels. He's new and he has no friends here. He's probably scared."

"Moose can't be scared," said Franklin. "He's so big."

Mr. Owl looked at Franklin. "Big or little, we all get scared."

Franklin thought about that.

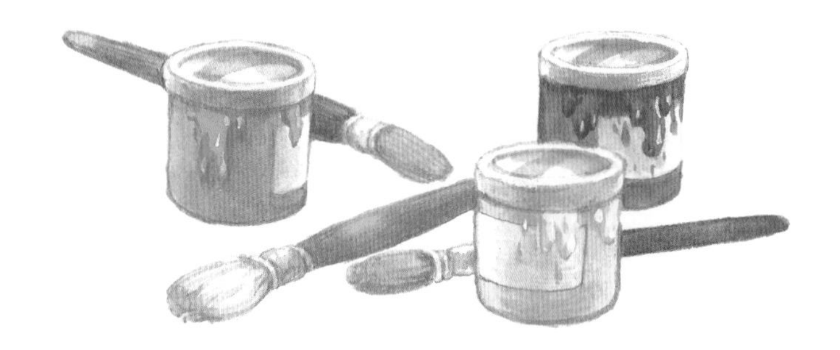

Franklin got the paints and the paper.

"Do you want to help me, Moose?"

"Oh yes," said Moose. "I love to draw."

They sat side by side and planned the poster together.

Franklin realized that Moose didn't seem as big when he was sitting.

After much work, the poster was perfect. They both thought so.

At library time, Franklin taught Moose how to borrow books.

Moose showed Franklin how to cut a perfect circle.

They both liked to build structures.

Franklin and Moose had a lot in common.

At lunch, Franklin made sure that Bear and his other friends got to know his new buddy.

They liked Moose. Besides, he was a very good soccer player.

When Franklin got home from school, he was happy.

"Guess what?" he told his mother. "I have a new friend."

"So you met Moose?" asked his mother. "What's he like?"

"Moose is big," said Franklin. "But he's not mean or scary."

"Good," said his mother. "Would you like to take some of these cookies to him?"

Franklin went to Moose's house. They ate all the cookies together.

"I'm glad you were my buddy," said Moose. "I was worried that nobody would play with me."

"Really?" said Franklin. He could barely remember being afraid of Moose.

From then on, Franklin and Moose played together all the time. Now Franklin's new friend was a special friend.

Franklin's Secret Club

Written by Paulette Bourgeois
Illustrated by Brenda Clark

FRANKLIN could count by twos and tie his shoes. He liked to play on teams and join in games. Franklin belonged to the school choir and the arts and crafts club. He liked belonging and that's why Franklin decided to start his own club.

One day Franklin discovered a hideaway near his house. It was the perfect place for a club.

"We can have a secret password and a secret handshake," Franklin told Bear.

"And secret snacks?" asked Bear hopefully.

"With secret ingredients," Franklin laughed.

The hideaway was very snug. It was too small for a big club.

"I know," said Franklin. "Snail and Rabbit will fit. Let's ask them to join."

Together, Snail, Rabbit, Franklin and Bear fixed up the clubhouse.

They called themselves the Secret Club.

The club members met every day after school. They ate blueberry muffins and made tin-can telephones. They made macaroni bracelets and gave them to one another.

Franklin was so busy doing secret things with the other club members that he almost forgot about the rest of his friends.

At school, everyone was being very nice to Franklin. Especially Beaver.

She saved Franklin a seat on the bus for three days in a row. She offered him the best part of her lunch. She even helped Franklin tidy up after art.

"Thank you, Beaver," said Franklin.

Beaver smiled. "Now can I join your club?"

Franklin was surprised. He didn't know that others wanted to join his club.

“Sorry, Beaver,” said Franklin. “But we can’t fit anyone else in the clubhouse.”

“That’s not a good reason,” muttered Beaver. “And it’s not fair. I’m going to start my own club.”

“But …” Franklin began, as Beaver left in a huff.

After school, Franklin's club had a treasure hunt.

Franklin didn't find a thing. He was upset because Beaver had been so angry.

"I told Beaver there just isn't room for more members," Franklin explained to Snail, Bear and Rabbit.

They nodded sadly.

The next day Franklin and Bear did their secret handshake – two slaps and a tickle – and whispered the password, "Blueberries."

Bear flapped his arms, wiggled his fingers, wrinkled his nose and said, "Fizzle-Fazzle, Diddle-Daddle, Ding-Dong-Bop!"

"What was that?" asked Franklin.

"The handshake and the password for Beaver's Adventure Club. Fox showed me."

"Oh," said Franklin.

The Secret Club members kept busy playing games.

Franklin had fun, but he'd heard that Beaver's club was even more fun.

"Today the adventurers are digging for dinosaurs," said Snail.

"The Adventure Club sure is amazing," sighed Bear.

"Sure is," said Franklin.

Franklin tried hard to think of secret things that were more exciting. The Secret Club members learned to write invisible letters with lemon juice, and one day they made a secret code.

But that very same day, the adventurers planned a trip to the moon.

Soon after, Franklin and his club members went to see Beaver's adventure headquarters.

There was a tree house to climb up to, a tire to swing from, a tent to play in and a big sign that said, "Members Only."

Franklin itched to join the Adventure Club.

"Now I know how Beaver felt," he said sadly. "Left out."

Suddenly, Franklin had an idea.

"Let's invite all the adventurers to join our club so *nobody* feels left out," he announced.

"But there's not enough room for everyone," said Bear.

"We can always meet outside," said Franklin. "Then there'll be plenty of room."

So Franklin invited Beaver to meet with him.

"I'm sorry I left you out," said Franklin.

Beaver accepted the apology. "I'm sorry that I left you out, too."

"The Adventure Club is a good club," said Franklin. "So is the Secret Club. But if we join together, we could have the *best* club."

Beaver agreed, and the two clubs became one.

Everybody was excited. Beaver's club members wanted to learn secret things. Franklin's club members were ready to explore.

The new club was called the Secret Adventure Club. Its password was Fizzle-Fazzle, Diddle-Daddle, Ding-Dong-Blueberry-Bop!

When the members greeted one another, they flapped their arms, wiggled their fingers, wrinkled their noses and did two slaps and a tickle.

Beaver made a sign for their club headquarters. It said, "Secret Adventure Club."

Franklin made another sign. It said, "Everyone Welcome."

He didn't want anybody to feel left out.